YO GABBA GABBA!

LET'S GET CLEANY-CLEAN!

ADAPTED BY JEAN MCELROY
BASED ON THE SCREENPLAY "CLEAN"
WRITTEN BY DAN CLARK
ILLUSTRATED BY PAUL ZDANOWICZ

SIMON SPOTLIGHT
New York   London   Toronto   Sydney

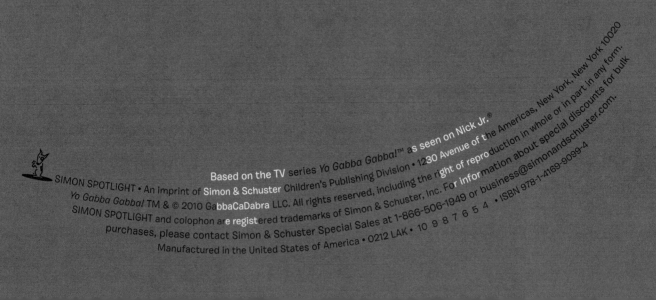

Based on the TV series *Yo Gabba Gabba!*™ as seen on Nick Jr.®
SIMON SPOTLIGHT • An imprint of Simon & Schuster Children's Publishing Division • 1230 Avenue of the Americas, New York, New York 10020
Yo Gabba Gabba! TM & © 2010 GabbaCaDabra LLC. All rights reserved, including the right of reproduction in whole or in part in any form.
SIMON SPOTLIGHT and colophon are registered trademarks of Simon & Schuster, Inc. For information about special discounts for bulk
purchases, please contact Simon & Schuster Special Sales at 1-866-506-1949 or business@simonandschuster.com.
Manufactured in the United States of America • 0212 LAK • 10 9 8 7 6 5 4 • ISBN 978-1-4169-9099-4

Hello, friends!
It's time to wash our germs away and get cleany-clean! Being clean makes everyone feel **super awesome**. Look! There are our friends! Let's see what they are up to!

"Hey, Muno! Let's play high five!" Toodee says.
"High fives are my favorite!" shouts Muno.
Cough! Cough! Muno covers his mouth.
Then Muno and Toodee slap hands.

"What are germs?" asks Toodee.

"Germs are tiny things that can make you sick!" replies Plex.

"But I don't want any germs," Muno says sadly.

"Put out your hands and I'll show you," Plex says.

He picks up a giant magnifying glass, and looks at their hands under the big glass. There are the germs! They are tiny and wiggly!

Here comes Foofa!
"Hi, Foofa! What are you
doing?" asks Toodee.

"I was planting pretty flowers in the dirt!
Planting flowers is so much fun!" replies Foofa.
Foofa claps her hands and jumps up and
down. Foofa loves flowers.

"Oh, no, Foofa!" exclaims Plex. "Flowers grow
in dirt, and dirt is full of germs!"
Foofa is not happy.
"Germs! What do germs look like?" asks Foofa.

Plex picks up his giant magnifying glass again. Through the glass Foofa could see lots of yucky, tiny, ugly germs on her hands!

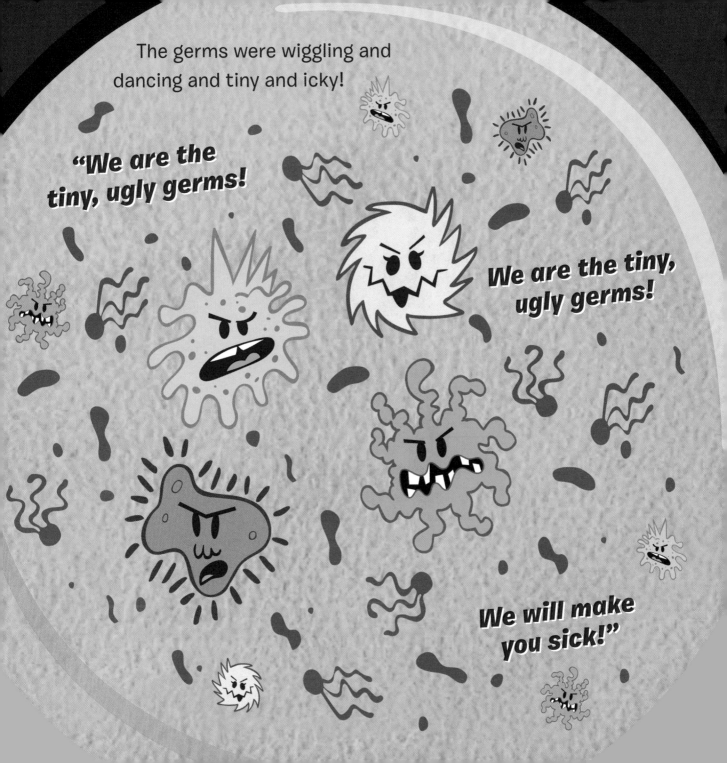

"Now can you see them?" asks Plex.

"Eww! Germs are icky and yucky!" exclaims Toodee.

"And they stick to you!" Plex says.

"What can we do to make these nasty germs go away?" asks Foofa. "I don't like them!" yells Muno.

DJ Lance tells them about a new friend, **Super Soapy Pal**. Super Soapy Pal is here to help the friends get cleany-clean!

Let's wash our hands and say good-bye to germs!

Super Soapy Pal tells the friends how it's done!

"With soap and bubbles and hot water,
we can send those germs right down the drain!"

"Yay! No more germs!" exclaims Muno.
"Thanks, Super Soapy Pal!"
The friends wave good-bye to their new pal.

Here comes Brobee!
Brobee is all dirty.
"Brobee, what have you been doing?" asks DJ Lance.

"I was playing in the dirt and now my hair is all yucky and stinky! What should I do?" asks Brobee.
"Oh no, Brobee! Dirt is filled with germs," says Foofa.

"Let's all shampoo!" Brobee declares.

DJ Lance gives everyone a few drops of magic shampoo.

Muno, Brobee, Toodee, and Foofa all rinse
off their foamy bubbles.

**"With soap and bubbles and hot water,
we can send those germs right down the drain!"**

"All the wiggly, yucky germs are gone," says Brobee. "And I smell great too!"

"YAY!" shout Toodee, Foofa, and Muno.

So, friends, don't forget to say good-bye to germs. When you're dirty and stinky, remember that **Super Soapy Pal** and **magic shampoo** are there to help wash those nasty germs right down the drain!

Being fresh and clean keeps you from getting sick and makes you feel super! It's much more fun to be **cleany-clean!**

PRAISE FOR *COLONUS*

GEEKIE AWARDS WINNER:
Best Art, Best Artist, Best Cover, Best Comic Book & Graphic Novel

"The dark dealings of politics in a compelling science fiction setting—best of both worlds that is perhaps the ultimate irony in this tale of planets at war!"

—JANE ESPENSON, *BUFFY, FIREFLY, BATTLESTAR GALACTICA*

"Big, expansive, filled with a rich curiosity of distant worlds and people, all of which become vehicles for examining humanity in its barest form."

—MICHAEL MORECI, *HOAX HUNTERS, ROCHE LIMIT*

"Bada bing! A mob war in space! Bad ass and righteous—even Tony's crew would not f*ck with these guys!"

—JOE GANNASCOLI, *THE SOPRANOS*

"*Total Recall* on steroids. If Frank Miller and Mike Mignola had a love child, his name would be Arturo Lauria. I'm drooling for the next chapter."

—MONKEYS FIGHTING ROBOTS

"5 out of 5 stars! Pisani creates a world that is so immediately believable that it's almost too scary to read. And speaking of horrific, Lauria's artwork is amazing and terrifying and compelling all in one."

—COMIC BOOKED

COLONUS

Created and written by **KEN PISANI**

Art by **ARTURO LAURIA**

Letters by **MAGNUS**

DARK HORSE BOOKS

president and publisher
MIKE RICHARDSON

editors
JIM GIBBONS AND **DAVE MARSHALL**

assistant editor
RACHEL ROBERTS

collection designer
BRENNAN THOME

digital art technician
CHRISTIANNE GOUDREAU

Published by
Dark Horse Books

A division of
Dark Horse Comics, Inc.
10956 SE Main Street
Milwaukie, OR 97222

DarkHorse.com
ColonusOnline.com
@colonusae
Facebook.com/colonusae

First edition: June 2016
ISBN 978-1-50670-121-9

1 3 5 7 9 10 8 6 4 2
Printed in China

Library of Congress Cataloging-in-Publication Data

Names: Pisani, Ken, author. | Lauria, Arturo, illustrator.
Title: Colonus / created and written by Ken Pisani ; art by Arturo Lauria.
Description: First edition. | Milwaukie, OR : Dark Horse Books, 2016.
Identifiers: LCCN 2016003667 | ISBN 9781506701219 (pbk.)
Subjects: LCSH: Graphic novels. | Science fiction comic books, strips, etc.
Classification: LCC PN6727.P487 C65 2016 | DDC 741.5/973–dc23
LC record available at http://lccn.loc.gov/2016003667

BUT MORE IMPORTANTLY:
THEY HAVE TO PASS EARTH

AT AN ALTITUDE OF 50 KILOMETERS, THE PRESSURE AND TEMPERATURE OF VENUS ARE PRECISELY EARTHLIKE.

AND IN A DENSE CARBON DIOXIDE ATMOSPHERE, A BREATHABLE OXYGEN-NITROGEN MIX HAS NEARLY AS MUCH LIFT AS HELIUM. ENOUGH TO SUSTAIN THE WEIGHT OF A CITY MIDAIR.

WE LAUNCHED OUR FIRST CLOUD CITY, *TIBERIUS*, JUST OVER A YEAR AGO. THE MARS COLONY TOOK IT AS AN "OPEN FOR BUSINESS" FLARE.

AND WITH THE RECENT DEPLOYMENT OF OUR NEWEST FLOATING CITY, *GAIUS*, THEY HAVE ARRIVED.

VENUS
3 MONTHS LATER

THIS IS AS CLOSE AS WE COME TO A *SACRED* DAY...

...WHEN ALL CITIZENS—EVERY MAN, WOMAN, AND CHILD— GATHER TO REMEMBER *THE FIVES.*

THE ONES WERE ASSIGNED AGRICULTURE...

THE TWOS, INFRASTRUCTURE...

THE THREES WERE TO EXPAND OUR CRITICAL AIR- AND WATER-GENERATING CAPABILITIES...

WHILE THE FOURS WERE TASKED WITH INCREASING THE SOLAR POWER THAT—SO CLOSE TO THE SUN—KEPT EVERYTHING RUNNING.

THE FIVES WERE SENT TO ESTABLISH AN IRON-MINING COLONY NEAR VENUS'S NORTH POLE...

THE LOSS OF *THE FIVES* WAS THE MOTIVATION THAT SPURRED US PAST MERE SURVIVAL...

TO HEIGHTS WE COULD NOT THEN HAVE *IMAGINED*.

TODAY, MEMORIALS TO *THE FIVES* ARE UBIQUITOUS.

Women on Mars are just one of many underclasses. We have **no** power, **no** voice. Just enough of us are allowed to **breed** as is necessary "for the good of the colony," and our children are taken from us at birth.

Those children are raised to perform hard labor, or serve as brutal law enforcement officers. They live their lives in **servitude**...and only the strong are allowed to breed again, perpetuating the next generation of workers.

Among the elite, wives are less than concubines—the women of our leaders don't even **live with them!** Instead, they live **communally**, with each other...in lavish conditions, but nonetheless reduced to outsider status.

Well...I admit some surprise to see three of my fellow citizens here at today's rally.

Much of what they say may sound shocking, but...well, we're different **cultures!** Should we be judged by the same values? Certainly there are aspects of Venus **we** could find fault with...

Wait, I agree...um, we need to address the concerns expressed here today.

I never said we had a perfect society! Perhaps we can learn from each other...and together, find the common ground for the betterment of **all** of us.

BOOOOO!

BOOOOO!

Thank you, no questions...

And since you made no attempt to deny the veracity of their stories...
...offering instead a stammering, "Yes, but nobody's perfect..."

25 YEARS
AGO

WHEN GRANDFATHER
DIED ALL OF VENUS
MOURNED

HE'D BROUGHT US TO THIS PLANET...

...AND SUSTAINED US THROUGH OUR HARSHEST TIMES,

HE'D LIFTED US FROM OUR WORST MOMENT, THE LOSS OF THE FIVES...

...AND LAID THE FOUNDATION FOR A FUTURE HE'D NEVER LIVE TO SEE.

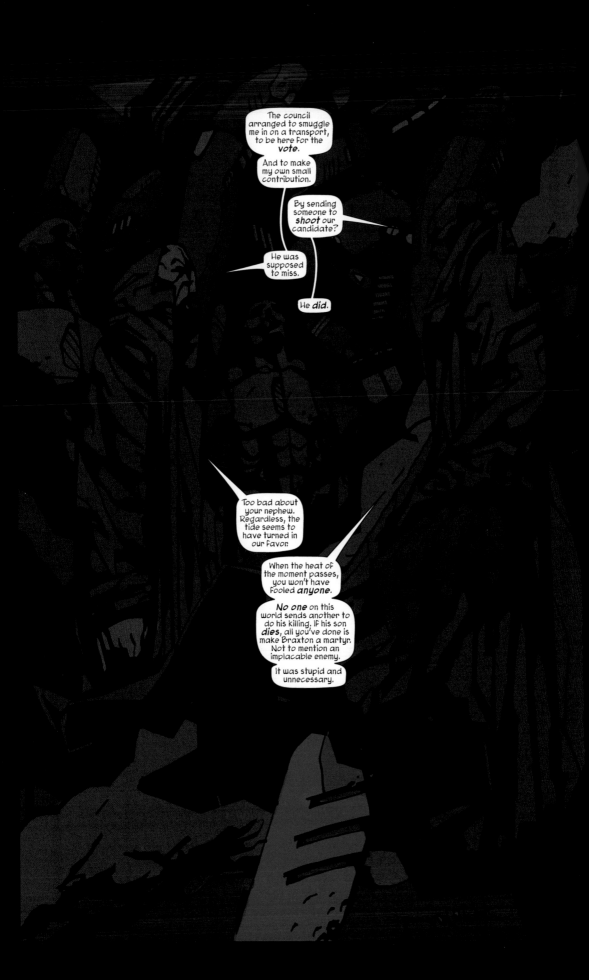

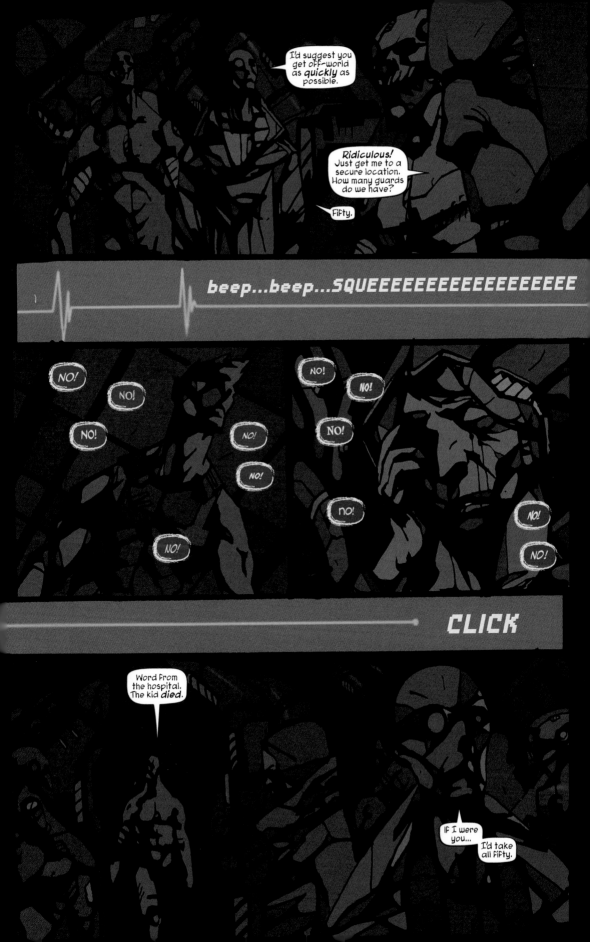

"Still groggy, Chancellor?"

"Take a few deep breaths...

"I want you fully awake for this."

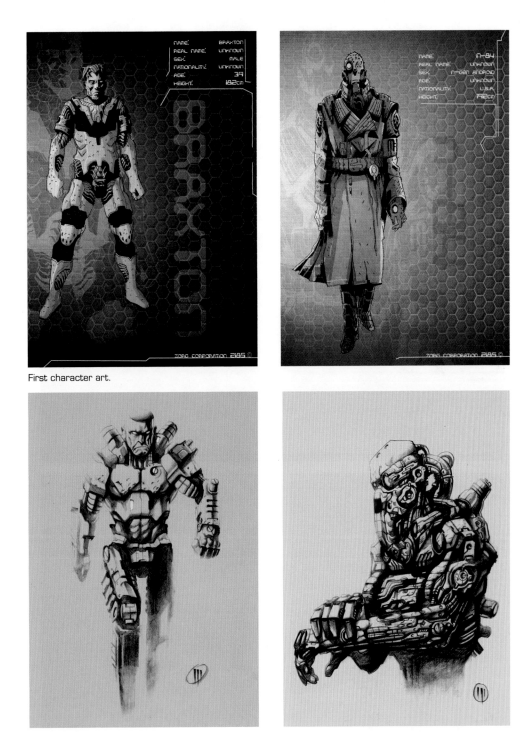

First character art.

Pencil sketches: exoskeletons and guards.

CHARACTER SKETCHES

The first drawings I got from Arturo were character sketches. (I remember how exciting it was!) I thought Braxton was pretty close to what I'd envisioned (my direction to him was "mid-40s, handsome and menacing, dark and shaggy . . . I'd like to see him look a little like Javier Bardem—but HANDSOME and RUGGED Javier Bardem, from *Biutiful*, not WEIRD SCARY Bardem from *No Country for Old Men*"). I thought the wardrobe was a little too sci-fi, so we dialed it down.

The next character sketch was problematic: Arturo sent me Android N-84 (!) instead of the Messenger. But it helped us focus on a key point moving forward: I wanted *COLONUS* to be plausibly futuristic— no androids, aliens, monsters, ray guns, teleportation, etc. That took care of Android N-84.

Arturo based Greer on one of his favorite comic book people, Grant Morrison.

D'oh! Wrong eye!!

Arturo's drawing table, where the magic happens!

WE NEED A VILLAIN

After killing off the Messenger, we needed an ongoing villain, and I asked Arturo to adapt N-84 for Greer. We kept the trench coat and the effed-up eye and made it part of his backstory—when Greer tried to kill him, Braxton stabbed him in the eye. But the eye created an early problem: Arturo kept forgetting which was his bionic eye, and we had to flip a couple of panels. (Note: I have to credit Arturo with the idea—after we'd already completed three chapters—to make Greer Braxton's banished brother. I loved it, and it was easy to retrofit into the story, amping up the Shakespearean family drama.)

Pen and ink: Braxton!

Braxton in brushes, guns, and armor.

PENS AND BRUSHES

When Arturo switched from pens to brushes, his style changed pretty dramatically—it got looser and more ominous. (You can see his art evolve from the opening pages through the final chapter.) These are some early pen drawings of Braxton, which he followed with his brush tests.

Venus underground.

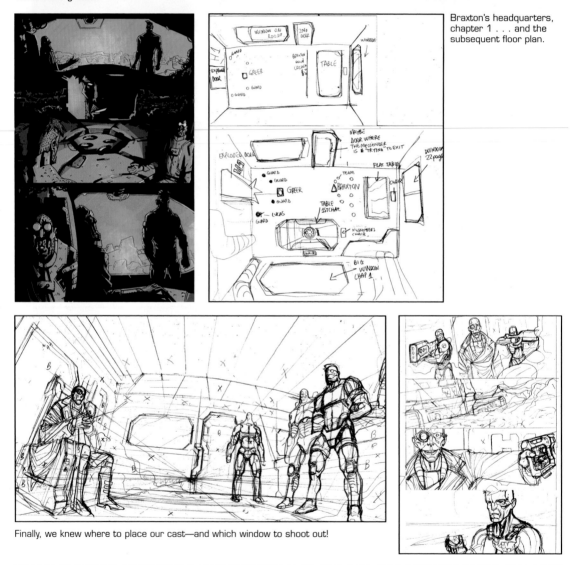

Braxton's headquarters, chapter 1 . . . and the subsequent floor plan.

Finally, we knew where to place our cast—and which window to shoot out!

BUILDING A WORLD
Arturo did a fantastic job creating Venus's subterranean look . . . but struggled a little with a specific recurring scene: Braxton's headquarters. We'd established it in chapter 1, but in later scenes I kept seeing pencils that didn't match at all. Finally Arturo made himself a floor plan of that central room, which helped a great deal and also helped me direct the scenes that took place there. (Illustrators, tear out this page and put it in your tips folder!)

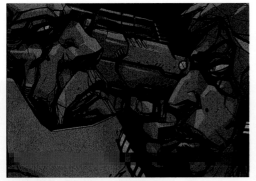

The ruthless Alameda makes a point.

The "Womancipators" of Mars!

Early sketch of a crew member.

Guns in faces!

WOMEN

With all the testosterone being sprayed by our main characters, it was very important to me that women also play important roles. Besides Braxton's ruthless mother, Alameda, we made sure that half of Braxton's lethal crew were women—as badass as the men. One of my favorite panels was Braxton's small female "protector" sticking her gun in Greer's face. It's a scene we mimicked later when Alameda shoves her handgun in another man's face. Nothing says equality like a woman with a gun in your face! The rebel women on Mars (dubbed "Womancipators") will figure very prominently in a future arc. And the standalone story "Last Dog on Mars" features another tough female protagonist.

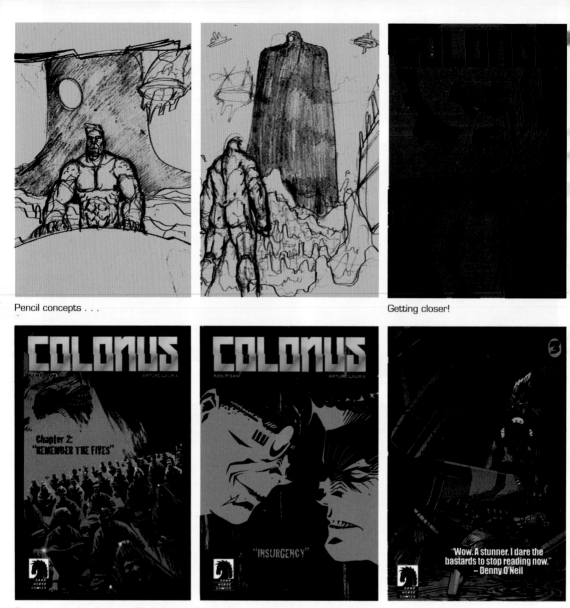

Pencil concepts . . .

Getting closer!

Promo covers for signings. (Of all the amazing blurbs we received from generous creators in comics, film, and television, this one from my boyhood comic book hero Denny O'Neil makes me want to weep with joy!)

COVERS

Arturo's first cover sketches were cool and ominous but a little inscrutable. I wanted more of a montage, while Arturo liked the idea of a single image. He eventually came back with the stunning black-on-red image—but it was a little too alien-looking (again, I didn't want the misdirect of aliens in space instead of human colonies). Also, while I loved his graphic two-color approach, Arturo is so good with colors that I felt this was too flat (it felt more like a cool poster than a cover). Arturo's final cover fixed both those things and kept that dangerous, ominous vibe. We later created these additional cover images for a limited signing when we debuted in *Dark Horse Presents*.